MINI SAGAS

THE ADVENTURE STARTS HERE 2009 ...

NEWBOLD COMMUNITY SCHOOL

First published in Great Britain in 2009 by
Young Writers, Remus House, Coltsfoot Drive,
Peterborough, PE2 9JX
Tel (01733) 890066 Fax (01733) 313524
All Rights Reserved

Disclaimer
Young Writers has maintained every effort
to publish stories that will not cause offence.
Any stories, events or activities relating to individuals
should be read as fictional pieces and not construed
as real-life character portrayal.

FOREWORD

Young Writers was established in 1990 with the aim of encouraging and nurturing writing skills in young people and giving them the opportunity to see their work in print. By helping them to become more confident and expand their creative skills, we hope our young writers will be encouraged to keep writing as they grow.

Secondary school pupils nationwide have been exercising their minds to create their very own short stories, using no more than fifty words, to be included here in our latest competition *The Adventure Starts Here 2009 ... .*

The entries we received showed an impressive level of technical skill and imagination, an absorbing look into the eager minds of our future authors.

CONTENTS

Alex Fullard (12) 1

Luke Wharton (12) 2

Shannon Hutton (12) 3

Nicola Fox (13) 4

Joel Gillham-Hardy (12) 5

Olivia Smedley (13) 6

Joshua Poole (12) 7

Chloe Rice (12) 8

Jordan Poole (12) 9

Jack Knapper (12) 10

Ross Stoppard (13) 11

Oliver Bates (12) 12

Sophie Armitage (12) 13

Laura Marks (12) 14

Sophie Middleton (12) 15

Josh Fields (13) 16

Jessica Hoskin (13) 17

Matty Singlehurst (12) 18

Jade Clarke (11) 19

Joe Barton (13) 20

Emily Skill (13) 21

Thomas Boden (14) 22

Shona Brown (13) 23

Lizzie Widdowson (13) 24

Luke Thompson (13) 25

Sam Rogers (11) 26

Matthew Boughey (12) 27

Ryan Mitchell (12) 28

Kirsty Barton (12) 29

Charlotte Lawless (12) 30

Charlie Mills (12) 31

Joseph Cocker (12) 32

Danielle Bramley (12) 33

Jack Barber (12) 34

Liam Chambers (13) 35

Corey Sargeson (12) 36

Becky O'Neill (13) 37

Amy Norton (11) 38

Abbie Thornton (12) 39

Emma Gibbions (12) 40

Jordan Bestwick (11) 41

Joe Turner (11) 42

Chloe Clarke (11) 43

Thomas Palmer (13) 44

Connor David Smith (13) 45

Heather Mason (13) 46

Ella Thompson (12) 47

Lori-Melissa Allen (12) 48

Hannah Preston (11) 49

Jack Woods 50

Liam Whetton (11) 51

Sophie Clarke (11) 52

Andrew Hopkinson (11)............................53
Ben Hague (12)......................................54
Connor Nelson.......................................55
Laura McLeavy.......................................56
Parrise Sheppard (11).............................57
Nathan Warby (12).................................58
Jessica Hallas (12) 59
Mollie Weeks (12)..................................60
Brogan Waterston (14)............................61
Megan Watts (13) 62
Ella Bramley (12) 63
Ashleigh Sellars (13)...............................64
Ashleigh Singlehurst (12) 65
Sharna Burdett (12)................................66
Dean Metcalfe (11) 67
Kelsey South (11)...................................68
Maisie Saikia (12)...................................69
Rebecca Sutcliffe (11) 70
Jordan Parsisson (11)..............................71
Remy Banks (11).....................................72
Bradley Hextall (11)................................73
Aimée Caton (11)...................................74
Jade Chaplin (12) 75
Sophie Eaton (13) 76
Louie Kierstenson (12) 77
Elizabeth Lloyd (11)...............................78
Kyle Robinson (11) 79
Holly Newton (12) 80
Joseph Taylor (12) 81
Ryan Shepherd (12) 82
Eleanor Gabbitas (12).............................83
Sam Genn (11).......................................84
Leonie Farrar (11) 85
Jack Dent (11)..86
James Bend (11) 87
Elisha Adin (11)......................................88
Chelsey Boaler (13)................................89
Leanne Perry (13)...................................90
Stephanie Forsyth (13) 91
Leah Simpson (13)..................................92
Joshua-Luke Higgins (11) 93
Chloe Wilson (11)..................................94
Kayleigh Harding (13).............................95
Libby Stoppard (13)................................96
Tammy Yeowell (13)................................97
Robert Taylor (13)..................................98
Melissa Walker.......................................99
Tom Bagshaw (13)................................100
Rebecca Edwards 101
Emily Handford (12)..............................102
Lauren Kirk (12) 103
Harley Ede (13) 104
Sophie Baker (12).................................105
Connor Christopher (13) 106
Sophie Mallen (12)................................107
Leah Mitchell (12).................................108
Natasha Pocock (12) 109
Bethany Lees (13)..................................110
Kerri Harwood (13)...............................111
Caitlin Garvey (11) 112
Tasha Booker (11).................................113
Danielle Jones (12) 114

Shawna Gibbions (12)....................................115
Ryan Pocock (11)..116
Jodie Maycock (11)..117
Curtis Myers (11)...118
Lindsey Hill (12)...119
Connor Smith (12)...120
Hannah Batteson (11)......................................121
Gaby Dakin (11)...122
Brydie Parkes (11)..123
Emily Heath (11)..124
Jamie Thelwell (11).......................................125
Jordan Cole (11)..126
Adam Elliott (11)...127
Kahn Davies-Collis (13)...................................128
Ruby Payne (11)...129
James Colls (12)..130
Bradley Goodall (12)......................................131
Chelsea Ryan (11)...132
Josh Wyatt (11)...133
Jacob Titterton (11)......................................134
Jack Harris (11)..135
Amy Goodwin (11)..136
Andrew Grafton (11).......................................137
Daniel Taylor-Beard (14)..................................138
Hannah Dickens (13).......................................139
Robert Dudley (13)..140
George Bates (13)...141
Joshua Wright (13)..142
Joel Williams (13)..143
George Foster (13)..144
Jake Alton (11)...145

Jack Morton (12)..146
Charlotte Stone (11)......................................147

THE MINI SAGAS

THE GRAVEYARD

It was a dark, misty night when five children were playing in a graveyard at night. They came across an empty casket on the path so they panicked. Suddenly, a mysterious figure rose from the ground. The children ran as fast as they could. Suddenly, complete silence struck the graveyard.

ALEX FULLARD (12)

BIG BAD GORILLA

Once upon a time, there was a gorilla called
Joe Young. His parents were shot when he
was young. He had to battle to survive against
poachers.
When Joe grew older, he was huge! The people
who lived around him raised enough money for
him to run around … but alone!

LUKE WHARTON (12)

2

IS IT A MONSTER?

Hayley felt a cold shiver run down her spine. Her breathing was getting heavier, her heart beating faster. She gasped and slowly turned around. The bush rustled. What was it? She slowly moved the branch then hesitated. A furry object brushed past her hand … a kitten! She gasped with relief.

SHANNON HUTTON (12)

THE FIGURE

Everywhere was blank, nothing in sight, only misty moorland all around me. Then, suddenly, a figure of darkness appeared, I panicked! I didn't know what to do. It felt like a cold knife ran down my throat. The figure came closer and there I saw a man …
Saved!

NICOLA FOX (13)

THE HOUSE

Creak, creak went the door of the abandoned house. Charlie entered the house, worrying what was lurking inside. A hand broke through the floorboards, Charlie ran but another hand and another came; he was trapped!
Bodies climbed out of the floor and bit Charlie. Charlie was now one of them …

JOEL GILLHAM-HARDY (12)

THE FLYING DUTCHMAN

I was floating up and down in the water, next to me was my boat. I turned to look where my oars were but I couldn't find them. Just then something grabbed my legs and dragged me down to the depths.
I now live on the Flying Dutchman forever!

OLIVIA SMEDLEY (13)

GHOST

It was all dark in Gary's house, his mum and dad
went to the shop, he was all alone, or was he? He
went into his bedroom and went on his Xbox but
his TV wouldn't work, he couldn't get it working
at all.
Suddenly, he cried out with fear!

JOSHUA POOLE (12)

JAWS!

There was a boy walking to his mum. The boy
asked if he could stay in the water. His mum said
that he could stay in for ten minutes.
Then he got eaten by the shark and it was like a
fountain of blood
Then his mum shouted his name!

CHLOE RICE (12)

WOLVES

Deep in the misty moorlands, where packs of wolves lived, each day a wolf would go out into the wild and fetch food for the other wolves in the pack.

The only problem with going out and fetching food was that you'd get chased by the farmer and his shotgun!

JORDAN POOLE (12)

THE CHIMP, THE GANGSTERS AND THE SWEET SHOP

'Hands on your head,' shouted the agent chimp,
just as he busted the gangster crew that broke
into the local sweet shop, stealing all the gummy
bears and white mice! The chimp handcuffed
them and took them back to the station.
'Lock them up,' Chimp said to the chief.

JACK KNAPPER (12)

INVASION

'Aliens, shouted my friend Bob. I looked up and there was a giant green disc. Suddenly a bright beam lifted me off the floor and into the disc. I woke up in a field. I flagged down a car and away we went … into another beam. Just my luck!

ROSS STOPPARD (13)

THE OBESE BOY

Once upon a time there was a boy and his family living very happily until Dave, started to eat all the time. Then his mum, Liz, started to notice Dave was getting obese. Dave realised he was putting weight on so he started to exercise, but he kept eating …

OLIVER BATES (12)

IT'S JUST A DREAM

'On your marks, get set, go!'
There I was, running the best I could. Hoping
to be first for my classmates. I didn't want to let
them down.
*What's this? I am first! They all run to me. They
cheer. They actually like me.*
Maybe not. I'd lost!

SOPHIE ARMITAGE (12)

THE TREASURE HUNT

Lily was on a treasure hunt with her friends, she
was walking along with her camera when she saw
a squirrel. She got her camera to take a picture
but the squirrel ran away. She put down her
camera and carried on with the hunt …
She won the treasure hunt!

LAURA MARKS (12)

THE MAN AND HIS DOG

There was once a crooked man named Zack. Zack once went to his local, scary, deep, dark forest with his pet dog, Albert. He let his dog off the lead. Later on he shouted for the dog, he didn't come back. What had happened? Would he come back?

SOPHIE MIDDLETON (12)

LOCK DOWN

As I entered the cold, dark basement I heard a sudden bang! The door had been locked from the outside. I had never been so frightened. The old cobwebs stared at me as I tried to find my way out. Then I saw a light but what was it … ?

JOSH FIELDS (13)

FEEBLE

I had seen this world. I had seen it well, I had understood this feeble existence, I had been given. I was not one to doubt fate or mock this life but now my existence would use its cruel hand and twist this knife, that would forever be my hindrance.

JESSICA HOSKIN (13)

BIN BOMB

It went off at exactly twelve hundred hours. It injured four, killed nine. There were terrorists all over the place. Then the police arrived and took them out, one by one.

There were bombs going off all over the place. Then the terrorists were all dead, the police tired.

MATTY SINGLEHURST (12)

THE SURPRISE PARTY

Ding-dong. 'Quick Sam, it might be Maisy, quick, hurry!'

'Fine, I'm going.'

Lilly opened the door with excitement but, unfortunately, it was only the milkman. Lilly was disappointed and sad. She thought everybody had forgotten her birthday.

Suddenly the doorbell rang. 'It's for you,' Maisy said ...

'Surprise!'

JADE CLARKE (11)

19

WHY ME?

I hadn't done anything wrong. I hadn't hurt them.
I don't think they cared. They just dragged me off.
I was too shocked to move.
Now I'm in a dark, damp cellar, with no
civilisation other than me and a grey rat.
Why me? I don't want to die …

JOE BARTON (13)

UNTITLED

Thomas was at school, trying to write his fifty-word story. He was frustrated, angry, ripping his hair out! Suddenly the page came alive, it grew and grew, then swallowed him whole!
'Hello, wake up!' yelled Miss Birtley at Thomas.
'Do you understand?'
'Yes, I've got the best idea ever!'

EMILY SKILL (13)

THE WEMBLEY KILLING

Me and my dad were going to watch England
against Germany. We arrived a bit late.
After ten minutes I went to the toilet, there was
a massive queue. When I came out there was a
crowd around my dad. I ran down and there he
was ... dead!

THOMAS BODEN (14)

I CAN'T DO IT

Shona is stressed. She doesn't know how to write
a fifty-word story. Well, she can, but she's getting
very stressed! She has Danielle moaning in her
ear. She's had it for fifty minutes now.
All Shona can think about is what she and Chloe
are doing after school!

SHONA BROWN (13)

UNTITLED

In the middle of the ocean, floating. All of a
sudden there was a great white shark! Ruby
was really scared, the ocean got rougher. Ruby
suddenly fell off her rubber ring.
She woke up to find that her little brother had
pushed her off the sofa.

LIZZIE WIDDOWSON (13)

DEAD RISING

The zombies had me surrounded. I used my gun
to kill some of them. I ran out of ammo. I ran to
the nearest shop in the shopping centre but there
were too many. I was bitten, dragged to the
floor …
I turned off the Xbox and went out.

LUKE THOMPSON (13)

LOST AND ALONE

The story is about three dogs that escape from their home. The pets get lost and must survive in the streets and woods of Chesterfield if they want to live. They will come up against tough challenges and foes to try and get home. It's a dangerous world out there.

SAM ROGERS (11)

HUNTED BY THE SHADOWS

The sky turned dark, shadows closed in, Sam
needed to escape but he couldn't!
The truth was inevitable, he would never make it
out alive. He could see strange shadows, as they
came closer, they looked like evil, bloodthirsty
monsters.
Then they closed in and he was never seen again!

MATTHEW BOUGHEY (12)

2000 YEARS AGO

Two thousand years ago in Italy, there was a small farm but it was no ordinary farm, it was abandoned! One tale tells that one man, brave and full-hearted, approached the farm, armed with nothing but a sword and a rusty shield. He opened the door to find … nothing!

RYAN MITCHELL (12)

28

FEAR!

As I opened the door, my heart throbbed with fear. I heard creaking from upstairs and then footsteps coming from my room. I went upstairs to see who or what was in my room. Slowly and quietly I opened the door and walked in. Then ... laughter from my baby brother!

KIRSTY BARTON (12)

THE HAUNTED HOUSE

There was a house that always creaked. The family that lived there was moving out because they had been hearing horrible sounds at night. But what they didn't know was the people moving in were not going to come back out the evil, haunted house.
The door slammed shut …

CHARLOTTE LAWLESS (12)

CREEPER

Suddenly a deep breath crept down the back
of my neck. I turned around, only to see a dark
space. I walked a few steps forward and I stopped
to notice the blood and drool on my shoulder. A
draught of cold rushed up my body. I looked up
... 'Argh!'

CHARLIE MILLS (12)

THE BIG SCARE

'What was that?' Joe asked.
'I'm not sure,' replied Lee, 'let's explore.'
So Lee and Joe crept deeper into the deep, dark
woods and started to explore. *Crack!*
'What was that,' asked Joe 'I think it's getting
closer.'
The bushes started to shake, twigs cracked …
'Manhunt, one, two, three.'

JOSEPH COCKER (12)

ME AND ALICE

Me and my mate Alice went to meet some
friends, it was pitch-black. We were walking
across the field and it was silent. We started to
run. Then Alice screamed when our mates scared
her.
We ran off the field then Alice screamed for the
second time ...

DANIELLE BRAMLEY (12)

A DAY IN AFGHANISTAN

We waited at the centre, the time … midday and
the Taliban were approaching. We fired the first
shot which wounded a soldier.
The battle started, a bullet hit me in the back, my
legs were frozen but the Taliban were retreating,
we had won the battle …

JACK BARBER (12)

TALIBAN TREASURE

One day I found a book, it led me to Afghanistan.
The Taliban captured me. They took me to their
leaders. The leaders were Bush and Obama. They
were trying to kill America! Soon they left.
I saw some treasure and a sword. They came in
and I killed them

LIAM CHAMBERS (13)

CHINATOWN BULLIES

There was a boy called Yamang Hu, he lived in China. He was bullied all the time but he used to fight back.

One day he went to school and told his teacher. She sorted it out and they all made friends. They all played football together.

COREY SARGESON (12)

HAUNTED HOUSE

There once stood a haunted house and only
Sophie McAndrew knew about it. This was how
she knew it was there.
Last summer she was cycling down the lane when
she saw someone coming from the chimney.
She went in to investigate. Inside she saw ghosts
and ghouls!

BECKY O'NEILL (13)

SEEING STARS

I was reading my horoscope one morning. It said, *Careful, you're in for a big hit.* 'OK, I don't get that, oh well,' I murmured.
I walked towards the door, still reading my paper when ... *bang!* I had walked straight into the wall.

AMY NORTON (11)

BOB THE DOG

It was snowing outside and Bob, the dog, wanted to go outside and play with the other dogs. His owner was asleep so Bob tried to go through the cat flap instead but got stuck. Poor old Bob was stuck there all night.
Eventually Bob's owner came and rescued him.

ABBIE THORNTON (12)

TONIGHT WE DINE IN HELL!

It wasn't the greatest day. A storm was brewing.
We knew it was going to last the night. We ate
and, suddenly, a lightning bolt struck the ship. The
rain flooded the ship. We weren't going to survive
the storm. We would have to dine in Hell with
something unexpected …

EMMA GIBBIONS (12)

THE VAMPIRE STRIKES BACK!

One night Pip was walking through the graveyard.
Something was moving in the shadows. He went
to inspect, there was nothing there, so he went
back to the path and carried on walking.
Swoosh! Out jumped a vampire, knocked Pip out
and sucked his blood. Was Pip dead ... ?

JORDAN BESTWICK (11)

41

BILLY

Billy was very adventurous. The police told him
not to go in caves on his own with no equipment.
But he didn't care. He went down caves, up
caves.
He loved them.
One day he went down a cave called Black Arrow
and broke his leg … He should have listened!

JOE TURNER (11)

ELLA

Ella was treated like a slave by her wicked stepmother. Ella found an invitation to the ball and went at 11.30pm. The prince saw 'love at first sight'. He asked for a dance.
At the end of the dance he asked Ella to marry him and she said, 'Yes!'

CHLOE CLARKE (11)

ASTHMA ATTACK

Steve had been given a trial for Chesterfield
Football Club. However, he had been living on
the streets and also suffered from a bad case of
asthma. He was having trouble breathing.
He had asked someone to buy him an inhaler.
They refused. Days before his trial, he passed
away!

THOMAS PALMER (13)

HALLOWE'EN HORROR

The children approached the dark and gloomy house at the top of the road. As they reached the house, the door creaked open and they saw a human-like figure in the house.

When they went in they saw that it was the owner, dressed as Dracula. 'Trick or Treat?'

CONNOR DAVID SMITH (13)

UNTITLED

A snap of a twig makes her jump. Her heart's
thumping louder, her eyes fill with tears. Fighting
her way through the woods, *'Help! Help!'* she
shouts. Her mouth dries and nothing's escaping.
Where am I? She wonders.
With a howl of a wolf, she passes out with fear.

HEATHER MASON (13)

THE TREE

Holly looked around, she was surrounded by green. Then she realised she was in the Christmas tree! She walked along as a bear ran past carrying presents.
Suddenly some baubles jumped down angrily. They forced her off the branch - she was falling
...
Holly shot up in bed. It was Christmas!

ELLA THOMPSON (12)

THREE, TWO, ONE, GO!

Three, two, one, come on, five laps, almost there!
Right, turn around and do backcrawl back, then
butterfly wiggle. Do breaststroke. One more lap,
come on.
Hi, I'm Nathalie, I'm swimming. I'm almost there.
I'm getting there, do rolls, Yes! I've won. I am
first! Wooh!

LORI-MELISSA ALLEN (12)

THE WICKED GIRL OF OZ

Elphaba was walking along the yellow road when
Dorothy, the wicked girl, tried to zap her with
her horrid little stick. 'Ha, you missed!' shouted
Elphaba.
'Well, I won't miss next time!'
Elphaba ran at speed into the castle. Magic doors
closed, 'I'm safe!'
Zap! went Dorothy. 'Now I've gotcha!'

HANNAH PRESTON (11)

WAREHOUSE

A monster lands on Earth into a giant warehouse.
The workers don't know what to do so they wait
for it to come out. The monster comes out and
gets scared and goes mad and tries to kill the
workers. They eventually kill it by cutting of its air
system!

JACK WOODS

JIMMY'S UNDERWORLD ADVENTURE

Jimmy was at the zoo eating some bananas when,
all of a sudden, a giant ape smashed out of his
cage. He started beating Jimmy to death.
Then Jimmy woke up in the Underworld next to
a snake, standing on two legs.
Then he got attacked by a piranha!

LIAM WHETTON (11)

REBECCA'S KOALA

Thirteen-year-old Rebecca goes on a holiday to
Australia and sees a stranded koala bear. Rebecca
decides to save the koala bear from the old
beach; she nurses it while she's there.
When it's time to go, her family decides to stay so
Rebecca can keep the koala bear.

SOPHIE CLARKE (11)

JONNY'S ZOO ADVENTURE

Jonny is walking around the zoo and hears an
announcement. 'A giant ape has escaped.'
The ape comes up behind Jonny, begins to punch
and kick him. Jonny gets up and goes. Then gets
jumped on by a tiger, is scratched and almost dies.
He gets up … then dies!

ANDREW HOPKINSON (11)

AGENT-T

Agent-T is a tiger, trying to foil Mucana's plans.
Mucana's got secret lairs on the top of a volcano.
One lair is called Castle-Octaveo.
Agent-T busts through the wall and gets trapped
in a cage. He finds a whistle and blows it and a
whale comes and help him.

BEN HAGUE (12)

UNTITLED

A wrestling match in New York City. It is the biggest fight of the century. This fight is amazing. It has new wrestling moves. If these two were a pair, they would beat up anyone in their way. Oh my God, there is blood everywhere. The ring ... it's horrible!

CONNOR NELSON

THE SPOILT DOG

Rocky lives in Paris. He is a spoilt dog, owned by
the Kelly family. Then they get a cat, Fluffy. Rocky
doesn't get a lot of attention so he finds a way to
capture Fluffy. The Kelly family sends out
a search.
Rocky feels responsible and finds Fluffy himself.

LAURA MCLEAVY

EGYPTIAN SPIES

This story is about two children, Max and Lola who are spies. They go to Egypt to defeat Evil. When they get to Egypt they stay in a little cabin and when Evil approaches they strike out. If they don't defeat Evil, then the world will come to an end!

PARRISE SHEPPARD (11)

WHEN ALIENS INVADE!

This story is about Jonny Smith and Tom Richards
and is set in New York.
Aliens invade and kill everyone in America, apart
from two members of the Army. They find
weapons and go onto the mother ship, plant a
nuclear bomb and wipe out all the aliens.

NATHAN WARBY (12)

UNTITLED

A hundred years ago there was a girl, Rachel, and
a boy, Tom, in New York City. They loved each
other but were both from a different religion.
One day they decided to run away together. They
had no idea where they were going but they said,
'Love is forever!'

JESSICA HALLAS (12)

BEAUTIFUL DAY

Sunbeams shone through the blinds on Sally Jones' bed. She woke and stretched. Opening the blinds she saw the sky was a brilliant blue. Sally could see the turquoise sea out of the corner of her eye.

Today was going to be a magical day.

MOLLIE WEEKS (12)

DEATH ON THE PLAINS

It was sunset but the heat was still stifling. The birds called out from their trees and animals gathered to drink from a lake. The Truman family watched from the safari car.
Suddenly the animals turned and ran in fright.
'What's the matter?' asked Tim.
They were his last words!

BROGAN WATERSTON (14)

THE SURPRISE

When I got home I noticed there were no lights
on, it was dark. I wondered why all my family
wasn't there on my birthday. I got to the door and
a note read, *Gone to Tesco*.
I opened the unlocked door and walked into the
kitchen … 'Surprise!'

MEGAN WATTS (13)

FRANK'S FRIGHT

Frank began to shiver as the cold winter's breeze
caught his neck. He could hardly breathe, he was
listening for any little noise.
Suddenly he heard footsteps coming from the
darkness outside his den. He crawled out to see
what it was, then felt something breathing
into his face ...

ELLA BRAMLEY (12)

LITTLE RED RIDING HOOD

Once upon a time there was a sad, lonely wolf
who longed for a little girl to be his friend.
Then lo and behold! Little Red Riding Hood came
into the woods and chased little, sad, lonely wolf
home!

ASHLEIGH SELLARS (13)

HOME ALONE AT NIGHT-TIME

I was walking home in the cold, groggy night. All of a sudden I heard a noise, so I walked faster, my heart beating faster. I got home to find a note, it said, *Tea in microwave. Back in a bit. Bang!* I heard a noise. I was scared!

ASHLEIGH SINGLEHURST (12)

MIDNIGHT

Star was walking in the wood. She didn't
know where she was going. She looked at her
reflection in the pool. Magically her reflection
spoke. It said, 'Jump into the water.' Star bent
her knees, jumping into the water,' her reflection
disappeared.
Star awoke, 'Oh silly me, I was dreaming!

SHARNA BURDETT (12)

THE DAY OF THE BOOM!

It was one dark and cold night, there was a *boom!*
In the night sky a star fell. I thought it was a sign
from Hell.
The ruins still remain of the blast but nobody
dares to pass. No one dares touch that star that
fell from the sky.

DEAN METCALFE (11)

UNTITLED

There was a beautiful girl, she was called Stella,
she had an ugly stepsister called Cinderella.
Cinderella's mother loved Cinderella but hated
Stella.
One day, every girl got invited to the ball but her
stepmother told Stella she couldn't go so she
sneaked there and the handsome prince chose
her!

KELSEY SOUTH (11)

THE CAVE

A sudden chill ran down Kathy's back as she entered the lost cave in her uncle's hidden cellar. It was the tiny speck of light that beckoned her to venture. Through the winding tunnel she trailed until she saw it! She couldn't believe her eyes ... Standing on a beautiful beach.

MAISIE SAIKIA (12)

NO ONE

There is a place where nobody goes, they all say
it holds one thousand souls from Hell below. The
trees are bare and the grass is dry. Does this place
exist. Are the stories true? Are the legends facts?
Nobody knows, nobody wants to know.
Nobody cares anymore!

REBECCA SUTCLIFFE (11)

UNTITLED

Bang! Clash! What was that downstairs? I walked down the creaky old staircase. I heard a strange noise coming from the kitchen. I was petrified! I slowly crept towards the door, the banging was getting louder and louder. I was extremely terrified … but it was only Mum dancing!

JORDAN PARSISSON (11)

UNTITLED

It was a cold, late night. The field was a dark
blanket of snow in the ghostly night. But in the
corner was a strange black figure. My face was
cold against the window.
The next morning I looked outside, it was there.
Mr Brooks still had his ornament outside!

REMY BANKS (11)

GHOSTLY GOINGS ON

One day, in the distant country of Africa, two children called Jermima and Jeremy were plodding home from a terrifying exam day at school.
When they got home, the lights were flickering on and off and their bedroom doors were creaking.
Then, there was a humungous crash!
What was it … ?

BRADLEY HEXTALL (11)

73

SHIPWRECK TREASURE

Beth and Harry are deep-sea divers off the
Egyptian coastline in the Red Sea. They come
across what looks like a pirate ship, with
a treasure chest.
Can they find the key and unlock the secret
treasure or does it unlock something else only for
pirates' eyes?

AIMÉE CATON (11)

HIDE-AND-SEEK!

It was getting dark. An owl hooted. My heart was thumping loudly behind my ribcage and all I could hear was my heavy breathing echoing within the hollow oak.

Suddenly fast footsteps approached. The owl's wings beat rhythmically through the cold air.

My older sister cried, 'I've found you!'

JADE CHAPLIN (12)

THE RACE

Heart pounding; beating faster. My body aching; legs quivering. Eyes stinging; gasping for breath. I double over, clutching my stomach in agony. Will I make it in time?

It's then I see it! Just out of reach … I begin to run again. It's getting closer. I'm running … Yes! I've finished!

SOPHIE EATON (13)

THE KNOCK

The house was empty. He was home alone. He heard a knock, but he knew that his parents were at work! The postman had been, so who could it be?
As he moved towards the door, the knocking got louder. He opened the door gingerly ...
there was no one there ...

LOUIE KIERSTENSON (12)

THE HORSE HORROR NIGHT

Charlie was just arriving at the North American horse ranch, to enjoy a night-time ride. She could faintly see in front of her, a horse skeleton. She started to wonder what was happening. There was blood dripping silently everywhere.
Then she saw Jane, the instructor, who exclaimed, 'Happy Hallowe'en!'

ELIZABETH LLOYD (11)

FUTURE

City Seventeen was plagued by evil creatures and the mayor didn't know what to do.

For some strange reason a man appeared and said, 'I can get rid of these evil creatures!' So the mayor employed him and … he failed!

The creatures enslaved the world and killed everyone!

KYLE ROBINSON (11)

THE PERFECT ADVENTURE

Australia is a big place, thought Gemma as she set out on an adventure to find a koala bear. She ran through heat, rain, cold and blazing sun. She battled crocodiles, spiders, snakes and lots more, only to find out that she was still in the zoo!

HOLLY NEWTON (12)

CHILDHOOD FRIEND

'*Argh!*' shrieked Josh, 'what was that?'
'Don't be such a Jessie,' replied Roger.
The two friends were inside a bloodcurdling
mansion, trying to find their lost friend. They'd
spent ages attempting to find him.
The last rusty knob, they turned and found ... the
rotten remains of their childhood friend.

JOSEPH TAYLOR (12)

BEAST QUEST

Carl went to the king and was given a quest to stop all evil beasts in North America (they were once good). So Carl set off to slay the dragon. Jason was standing next to Krurg, the dragon, waiting for Carl.
As Carl came, the dragon charged at Jason …

RYAN SHEPHERD (12)

THE NOISE

Click, click! Amber returned home but there was
a ghostly presence as she shut the door! *Scratch,
scratch!* 'What was that? Come out whoever you
are!'
Slowly turning the broom cupboard doorknob,
something sprung onto Amber, knocking her
down!
'Scruffy!'

ELEANOR GABBITAS (12)

THE HAUNTED HOUSE

Holly walked up to the steel gates; they creaked as she opened them. She ran up the path leading to the mysterious house, she could hear the bats squeak. She reached the huge door and knocked on it. A vampire answered and said, 'Hi Holly, glad you could come!'

SAM GENN (11)

MIA

Mia and her twin sister were walking down the deserted road when they heard a rustling. Mia looked back. When she looked forward, Maya was gone and a ghost was staring her down ... It was her sister. 'Mia wake up, it's Christmas,' her sister screamed in Mia's ear!

LEONIE FARRAR (11)

THE EVIL CHOCOLATE

There was a good boy called Snooty who
was dead rich. He was looking for his sweet
chocolates. After they went missing, he felt
dripping hot chocolate up his sleeve. It was a
chocolate holding a sharp knife.
The sun was red-hot and melted the sweet
chocolate away.

JACK DENT (11)

HAUNTED

A nice, kind boy called James, saw this old house and investigated. A creak of the door as it opened. A ching of a knife. Footsteps, then a thumping on the dark creaky stairs. James turned, then …

'Boo!' his dad went.

Argh!' James screamed. the house wasn't haunted at all!

JAMES BEND (11)

LOST

Dear Diary, I've been locked in this freezing cellar
for three days. I'm starving, practically wasting
away. I'm only down here because my brother
has locked the door. Everybody's out there
looking for me, worried, he knows where I am.
Pitter-patter, pitter-patter.
'Argh! It's coming.'

ELISHA ADIN (11)

SURPRISE!

Hi, my name's Talky, it's not my real name
though.
I walked into my house one day and it was dark.
The next thing, I heard someone whispering.
Then ... 'Happy birthday!'
Scared me half to death. I never had a clue. There
was all my family!

CHELSEY BOALER (13)

HELP

Alone, nobody to sit with or talk to. Shall I smile
at somebody? No, maybe not. Will I get smacked
after school again, like last week? I can't tell
anybody …they'll get me.
'Oi, Rosie! Homework now!' said Becky.
'Pick on somebody else for a change and leave me
alone.'

LEANNE PERRY (13)

MISSING!

As Tom's parents set the table, decorated the house with banners and balloons, they answered the door to several people that turned up to the party.

As they nervously answered the door, they were shocked to see a policeman. He whispered, 'I'm sorry but your son has been kidnapped!'

STEPHANIE FORSYTH (13)

MIAOW

'Help, oh help!' I sit in the corner and cry. I'm scared on my own and in the dark. The door from the downstairs living room opens. I hear footsteps. The floorboards creak. The door opens … *Miaow!*

LEAH SIMPSON (13)

BIG, GREEN AND EDIBLE

In North America, at the stroke of midnight, little Lucy went for a wander. She went over the hills and into the forest …

All of a sudden, a green blob tried to eat her and … it did! Soon she realised it was made of jelly and she ate it!

JOSHUA-LUKE HIGGINS (11)

THE SPOOKY MUM

A cold night, there were two boys called Jake and
Nike, they were in bed when they heard some
sounds. They said, 'Ghost! *Argh!* There is a ghost!
Help!' So they went to see.
In the end it was their mum. 'She's not scary is
she?'
'No!'

CHLOE WILSON (11)

HALLOWE'EN

Knock, knock! I heard the door, pulling myself away from the TV, I crept over to the door and peered through the peephole. I opened it to blood-smeared faces, staring cunningly at me with big grins on their faces. Their clothes viciously, ripped, 'Trick or treat?' they screeched.

KAYLEIGH HARDING (13)

UNTITLED

'It's time, I'm sure it is,' Izack said in excitement.
'*Shhh!*' another voice said from the dark room.
'Something's on our roof,' Emily cried out.
A loud bang came from down the stairs. Jingles
ran through their ears. Happiness filled the room.
'Yeah, Santa's here,' giggled Izack.
The children smiled.

LIBBY STOPPARD (13)

MILLY AND MIA GET LOST

Molly and Mia decided to go to the woods for a walk. When they got there, Mia heard a noise, they were scared to look back. They both ran off the footpath into the wood. They were lost. When they got home they were told off and sent to bed.

TAMMY YEOWELL (13)

THE WIN THAT KILLED ME

I was surrounded, I recognised one of them. It was the guy I beat yesterday at Motocross for the title. They had knives. I ran. One of them laughed at me, tripped me up and put a knife to my throat.

RIP Rob Taylor.

ROBERT TAYLOR (13)

UNTITLED

Melissa was walking home from school when a man in a van waved to her. She was minutes away from her house. When she arrived at her house she could hear people inside. She was so scared. She felt a sudden relief when her mum arrived home.

MELISSA WALKER

DRAGON SLAYER

Ash ran out of his castle with his sword held high.
He was prepared to fight the dragon. He blocked
some fire with his shield, his helmet wobbled,
then someone spoke, 'Ash, take that bucket off
your head and wash the dishes. Kids!' she said.
What a dragon, Ash thought.

TOM BAGSHAW (13)

UNTITLED

Kiki and Tarb prepared for battle. They had lost too many comrades to Rider and her army of Shadow Mutants. Kiki and Tarb ran to the battlefield and fought with all their might. After hours of fighting, the war was over and Kiki and Tarb had won!

REBECCA EDWARDS

THE LOST WAR

She stood in the middle of the field. The rain splashed onto the ground. Dark figures rose over the hill. Men rose on the other side.

They started charging towards her and were carrying heavy metal rifles. She thought she would die; they stopped.

It was a war re-enactment!

EMILY HANDFORD (12)

NOISE

Bang! Bang! Bang! Bang! It was silent for a moment
then ... *'Argh!'* Amy-Mai ran down the hallway,
slamming the door open and peeping around the
corner. The sight was horrific ...
it was her brother on his new DS game!

LAUREN KIRK (12)

DRAGON WARRIOR

It was early one morning and Jack had to deliver noodles around town when he realised it was the kung fu festival.
He ran to the top of the hill as fast as possible.
Someone was chosen every one thousand years to defeat the evil wart …
He was named Dragon Warrior!

HARLEY EDE (13)

DEEP IN THE WOODS

It was dark and gloomy as Charlotte walked through the woods. Suddenly she heard a crack as a twig broke. She started running faster and faster. She could hear another set of footsteps.
Then she stopped ...
'Boo!'
She jumped, it was only her best mate, Jordan.

SOPHIE BAKER (12)

UNTITLED

It was the 25th December 1942. A tramp was walking along when a man took him to Everest. The man was famous. He forced him to climb the mountain so they both did. The tramp got to the top and died, The other died along the way!

CONNOR CHRISTOPHER (13)

LITTLE REBEL RIDING HOOD

Rebel set off to Granny Patsy's cottage, she arrived, glaring at an ugly face, poking outside the duvet. Rebel said, 'You again!' This time Rebel came prepared and *bang!* Wolfie was gone! Rebel rescued Granny from the cupboard and used the wolf skin for a new wolf-skin coat!

SOPHIE MALLEN (12)

UNLUCKY

Jane was at the factory. Like any other day, Owen had checked the machines, so Jane went and sat down. She was putting books in a machine so that they would stay together. It didn't seem to be working.

Then suddenly, *bang!* A massive staple pulled her finger straight off!

LEAH MITCHELL (12)

GOT YOU!

Four girls are getting into the pool, ready for a swim. One of the girls is a professional underwater swimmer, Lily. Lily pretends to drown. The others get worried and try to help her.

After a while she jumps out and says, 'I got you all!'

NATASHA POCOCK (12)

THE THING

I ran through the pitch-black corridor, trying to get away from the thing that was after me. Its slimy hand grabbed my face and pulled me down. This was the end, I was trapped.
I lifted up my head … various Cheerios stuck to my face. I'd fallen asleep again!

BETHANY LEES (13)

A BIRTHDAY IN THE CLASSROOM

As Caitlin walked down the corridor her heart raced. This was the worst thing she had ever done. Caitlin knew that as soon as she opened the door, everyone would cheer, and they did! She sighed and looked at her friend for help. 'Happy birthday, Caitlin!' everyone shouted, clapping hard.

KERRI HARWOOD (13)

THE TV OF DOOM!

The TV started to glow green, a screeching sound came from within it. 'Throw a book at it,' Lucy screamed.
'Help, it's gonna blow,' Yasmin screamed as popcorn flew over her head.
'I've broken a nail,' Lucy cried.
But the glow turned red and they were sucked in!

CAITLIN GARVEY (11)

HAPPY BIRTHDAY LUCY!

'Wake up, wake up, Mum, it's Lucy's birthday'.
'OK, OK, don't panic Tasha. First I will get the
food, you will get the cake,' Mum shouted.
After an hour, Lucy knocked on the door, there
was no reply. She entered the room ...
'One, two, three, Happy birthday, Lucy!'

TASHA BOOKER (11)

SHOCKER!

An investigation trip, *wow!*
In a cave, it was dark and gloomy. My teacher
said we were investigating a crime. We split up,
holding a torch. Strange sounds! To my horror a
zombie stepped out … *'Argh!'* The head came off.
It was only my teacher, *phew!*

DANIELLE JONES (12)

THE MAGICAL SURPRISE

Kirsty was waiting for her birthday, counting down the days, she couldn't wait. She was in her room, she could hear a sprinkle, she felt her room starting to change! What was happening? It was her birthday, yes, for some reason she fell asleep ... thanks to ... well, she'll never know!

SHAWNA GIBBIONS (12)

ONE CHRISTMAS

Callum was getting worried. His presents weren't
under the tree. Had Santa forgotten him?
'Of course he hasn't, Callum,' his dad told him.
By this time Callum was crying. He fell to sleep.
When he woke up in the morning he was
surprised to see all his wonderful presents!

RYAN POCOCK (11)

THE DARK, DARK WOODS

Jelly, Bob and Fran were out looking for their pet dog, Wolfie. As they were walking, they heard something rustling. They just ignored it and walked away. Suddenly something jumped out and licked them. What was it?
It was only Wolfie saying hello to them!

JODIE MAYCOCK (11)

CLOWN

There were two boys who were best friends called James and Curtis. They decided to go to the circus, aka Johnny's circus. There was Johnny selling balloons so Curtis and James went to get one and when they got one, it transported them into a black hole. Watch this space …

CURTIS MYERS (11)

MOST HAUNTED

I was with my friend in her living room, we were watching Most Haunted. Then the door opened on its own! We both freaked out! We looked but nothing was there ...

LINDSEY HILL (12)

TROY, THE NEW VERSION

Greeks decide to invade Troy. Troy holds them by using force and guns and lightsabers. Greek soldiers kill Trojan prince by fighting in the WWE. Greeks use helicopters to get inside the Trojan walls. They get inside and use bombs to defeat the Trojans. They burn down mighty Troy.

CONNOR SMITH (12)

DING-DONG, IT'S HALLOWE'EN

Ding-dong! Harriet and Holly jumped up, shaking. It was twelve o'clock, midnight. Nobody was around then. They ran to the door and turned the key ... 'Trick of treat?' Their faces dropped in horror.
There, standing at the door, were dripping fangs and torn skin ...

HANNAH BATTESON (11)

A NASTY SURPRISE

'Happy birthday,' shouted my mum. The only
thing wrong was it was my worst enemy's
birthday too.
'Come on, Rosie, guests will be here soon.'
'Guests?' I replied in astonishment.
When I got there nobody was there apart from
my worst enemy Jim. What was I supposed to do?

GABY DAKIN (11)

LOLA

Lola was a brave girl. One day she had a mission
to fetch a golden arrow from the top of Mont
Thon.
Up, down, up, down. Lola swung up and *crash!*
The golden arrow, mission accomplished.

BRYDIE PARKES (11)

MY FAMILY

My name is Chloe Mae and I'm forced to live in this stupid magical land by my stepdad, who is a wizard. I also live with my mum (she is not magically inclined). I also live with my half-sister. She is horrid and that's my family.

EMILY HEATH (11)

ROBIN HOOD

He walked, scared but brave, into a dark and
gloomy wood. Robin Hood was a stealing man, he
stole from the rich and gave to the poor.
The mayor was at war with him, he was looking
for him. 'Hey, he is there, get him!'
He was dead meat!

JAMIE THELWELL (11)

DING-DONG, IT'S JACK'S BIRTHDAY

Ding-dong, it was Jack's birthday and Hallowe'en.
Jill and a devil were behind the door. Jack went
into the kitchen. Jack got scared.
They all shouted, 'Surprise!'

JORDAN COLE (11)

TRAPPED

Walking through the woods, Jamie finds a house.
Through the creaking door, up the squeaky stairs,
he wanders along the landing, scared stiff. He
falls down into the cellar, the door slams shut.
Screaming 'Help!' he comes upon a sign, *Happy
Hallowe'en!*
He stands there in horror. He is trapped!

ADAM ELLIOTT (11)

ELEPHANT, ELEPHANT

(My version of Tom Jones' 'Pussycat, Pussycat')

'Elephant, Elephant, where have you been?'
'I've been to London to sit on the Queen.'
'Elephant, Elephant, what did you do there?'
'I squashed poor Pussycat under the stair!'
'Elephant, Elephant, why'd you come back?'
'I only came back because of the cat.'
'Elephant, Elephant, I'm glad you're back.'

KAHN DAVIES-COLLIS (13)

THE CHRISTMAS DREAM

One Christmas Eve night, a girl called Amy was asleep. Suddenly she heard a creak downstairs. She went to investigate. She went downstairs and, stunningly, a huge figure appeared. It was Santa. She knew she should be in bed but Santa still gave her a present.

RUBY PAYNE (11)

SCARY CHRISTMAS

I was in my house on Christmas Eve. It was
eleven o'clock. I heard a 'Ha, ha, ha', and
something glowed outside. I went outside with
a torch, then I found out it was my dad's broken
Santa.
I woke my dad so he could turn it off!

JAMES COLLS (12)

CHRISTMAS NIGHTMARE

There was a creak upstairs. Josh went upstairs
and he went to his bedroom and looked in his
mirror. He saw a yellow man warning him, 'Don't
open the door!'
Josh took no notice and opened the door.
He fell downstairs and died!

BRADLEY GOODALL (12)

KERRI'S DAY

I walked through the front door. I was screaming
because it was my birthday on Hallowe'en. It was
silent, nobody was there. Then a noise came from
the cellar. I crept down and a witch jumped out
and shouted, 'Happy birthday.'
It was Mum, along with friends and family.

CHELSEA RYAN (11)

THE BOMB OF EVIL

Tom and Harry went to a hill, it was dark. The trees were covering all the sky. Suddenly there was an ear-piercing bang and the screaming of sirens. A black screen of dust covered the land. The dust cleared but everywhere were screams of people shouting for help.

JOSH WYATT (11)

THE HAPPY HELPING DIGGERS

Tessie and Grumpy were lovely little dogs until one day their owners left the door open. They found themselves in a big dump. Happy Digger found them and gave them back to their owners. 'Well,' said the owners, 'you two really need a bath!'

JACOB TITTERTON (11)

HELL'S HIGHWAY

Hell rises from the Earth and evil starts to spread all over. The army tries to stop it but nothing works. I think the Earth is in panic mode. The Earth will be lost in a matter of hours. The Earth will have to fight …

JACK HARRIS (11)

THE SCARY SURPRISE

Millie and Rory walked through the door, not a
sound. *Creak, creak* went the floorboards. 'I am
scared,' said Millie.
The door flung open. Two big, furry feet peeped
around the corner … 'Happy birthday,' shouted
friends and family.
'What a lovely surprise. Wow, what a good
surprise!'

AMY GOODWIN (11)

CREEPY CHRISTMAS

It was Christmas Day and Tom had just woken up, he jumped out of bed and ran downstairs. 'That's strange!' he said. He started to look round for everyone in the house but there was nobody about. Suddenly his family leapt out and made him jump …
'Argh!'

ANDREW GRAFTON (11)

INSPECTION

Mrs Turtles cautiously opened the staffroom door and standing before her were three daunting figures. They had their glasses on the peak of their nose; one of the figures muttered, 'Mrs Turtles, your school has passed the inspection.' Then Mrs Turtles couldn't contain her excitement and smiled with joy.

DANIEL TAYLOR-BEARD (14)

TRICK OR TREAT?

Kimmy and Alice were going trick or treating. They came to a house, *knock, knock, knock* ... The door swung open, it was very dark; they heard footsteps. They said to each other, 'Guess it's a trick!' They walked down the drive to the gate and it opened by itself ...

HANNAH DICKENS (13)

A GHOSTLY ENCOUNTER

The faces looked at me from all around. They were monsters from another world, and I just couldn't escape. They let out an evil cackle, they were determined that I had been trapped.
Five minutes later, I could see the light. 'I'm never going in a ghost train again!'

ROBERT DUDLEY (13)

TRAPPED

He entered the room, it was dark and hot. As he
walked further on in he found a television. He
went to turn it on and the door slammed shut,
he was trapped! The door was solid shut as he
kicked and punched it ...

GEORGE BATES (13)

THAT'S WHAT YOU GET FOR RUNNING OFF!

One morning Dave went to his friend's house and
he said, 'Hey, come on, Harry, let's run away.'
'OK,' said Harry.
That evening they packed a bag each and set off.
They were running away until Dave fell down a
hole. 'Oh God,' screamed Dave …
So much for running away.

JOSHUA WRIGHT (13)

PRESENTS

It was Christmas Day and Alan rushed downstairs to discover there were no presents. *Where are my presents?* he thought. His parents came down and he told them about it. Then he saw the presents, under the tree as usual.

JOEL WILLIAMS (13)

IT WAS ALL A DREAM

John fell out of bed and went straight through the floor. He landed with a crash. He got up and opened the front door, it fell off. He turned round, walked up the stairs and he fell through them too.

Then … he woke up!

GEORGE FOSTER (13)

SAUSAGE

Beep, beep, beep, beep. The noise woke him instantly, constant beeping. Even though he was shocked, he still ran to the door. Slowly he opened the door, no fire there. As he made his way along the corridor, he heard it, 'Breakfast's ready, bit burnt though!'

JAKE ALTON (11)

SPLATS OF BLOOD

Jason wandered through the deserted woods.
The trees cast shadows across the floor. *Snap!*
Jason turned, only to see the trees and plants.
Splat! Splat! Splat! Blood splats hit the trees,
then Jason. Jason turned again and saw heavily
armoured soldiers. 'You're out,' shouted a soldier.
Jason's paintball game was over!

JACK MORTON (12)

THE PIED PIPER OF CHESTERFIELD

Rats everywhere. The mayor is being selfish. The townsfolk are protesting. The mayor is overjoyed when he sees the strange figure of the Pied Piper. He plays his pipe and drowns the rats in Tapton Lock.
'Now I'll take the children,' he shouts and he takes them up the mountain …

CHARLOTTE STONE (11)

INFORMATION

We hope you have enjoyed reading this book - and that you will
continue to enjoy it in the coming years.

If you like reading and writing, drop us a line or give us a call and
we'll send you a free information pack. Alternatively visit our
website at www.youngwriters.co.uk

Write to:
Young Writers Information,
Remus House,
Coltsfoot Drive,
Peterborough,
PE2 9JX

Tel: (01733) 890066
Email: youngwriters@forwardpress.co.uk